TWO TINY MICE

ALAN BAKER

Dial Books for Young Readers · New York

Two tiny
field mice,
look out
into the world.

They see
a soft,
furry rabbit
resting in
the sun,

a big March hare,

and a shuffling, snuffling mole.

They see
the shy,
little
sparrow
in its nest
of twigs,

and a sly,
old fox
far up
on the hill.

Two tiny
field mice
look again
and see

a croaking frog,

a quacking duck,

a weasel
at the
river's edge,

and a
muddy-brown
otter
swimming
in the water.

Two tiny
field mice
look
once more
and see

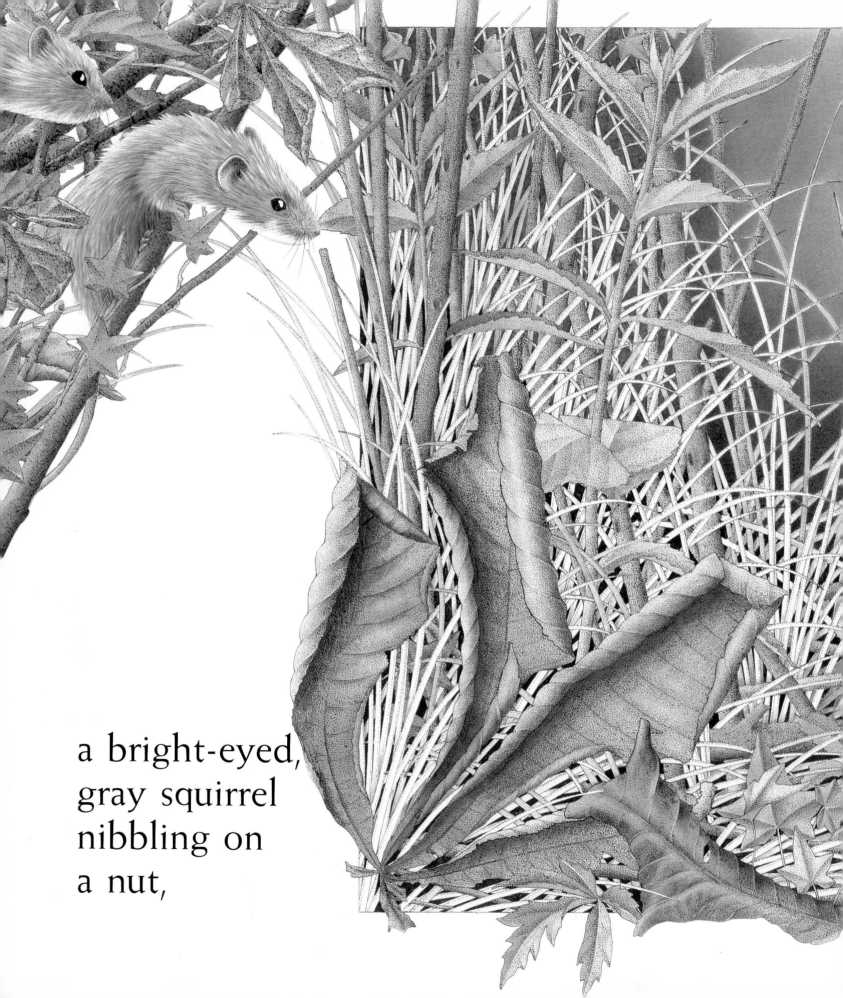

a bright-eyed,
gray squirrel
nibbling on
a nut,

a spiky,
spiny hedgehog
rustling through
the leaves.

But
do they see
two badgers,
playing
in the dark?

NO . . .

Two tiny field mice are home and sound asleep in their nest.